THE BLUE GIANT

KATIE COTTLE

Text and illustrations:
Katie Cottle © 2020

Publisher: Neil Dunnicliffe
Editor: Hattie Grylls
Art Director: Anna Lubecka

First published in the UK in 2020 by Pavilion Children's Books,
43 Great Ormond Street, London, WC1N 3HZ.
An imprint of Pavilion Books Company Limited.

ISBN: 9781843654513

A CIP catalogue record for this book is available from the British Library.

10 9 8 7 6 5 4 3 2

Reproduction by Mission, Hong Kong.
Printed and bound by Bell & Bain Limited, UK.

This book can be ordered directly from the publisher online at
www.pavilionbooks.com, or try your local bookshop.

THE
BLUE
GIANT

KATIE COTTLE

PAVILION

Meera and her mum are heading to the seaside.

They're looking forward to a day on the beach and a trip in their little boat.

But just as they start to relax,
something strange happens.

The sea gets restless. There is a low rumbling and then...

Out of the blue rises

a great big **giant**,

who seems to be made of the sea.

It makes a gurgling noise, as if it
has something important to say.

And then in a splashy voice it says,
"I have a message from the ocean.
We really need your help!"

Meera and Mum climb aboard their boat and follow the giant.

They plunge into the sea.

All seems quiet until...

...the giant swirls and splashes

and shows them just how much

R U B

B I S H there is all around.

Meera and Mum start to clear up the mess,

helping each creature one by one.

It's a **huge** problem.

Animals and birds that live above
the waves are affected, too.

"Thank you for making a start," gurgles the giant.
"With your help we can clear up this problem."

There is a lot more work to do.
It won't be easy and it's too much for two people.

The next day, Meera returns to the beach and begins picking up as much litter as she can.

She does it the next day,
and the next, with friends...

...and friends of friends!

Each good deed, and act of kindness inspires the next.

And when everybody helps out...

...even the **biggest** messes can be fixed!

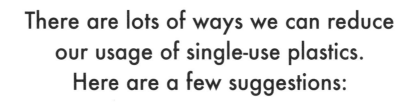

There are lots of ways we can reduce
our usage of single-use plastics.
Here are a few suggestions:

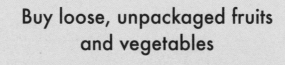

Buy loose, unpackaged fruits
and vegetables

Switch to a bamboo toothbrush

Use solid, packaging-free
cosmetics like bar soap
and shampoo bars

Drink with reusable
or paper straws

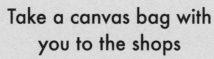

Carry a reusable water
bottle/coffee cup

Take a canvas bag with
you to the shops

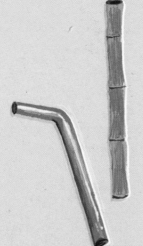